Rosie liked gossip, other people's that is, but not if it was about her.

"How's Morris? Is it true he's in prison?" asked the fishmonger's wife.

"What concern is it of yours? Mind your own business."

She grabbed the herrings wrapped up in newspaper and left.

"Cheeky bugger!"

Of course Rosie knew that her brother, Morris, was serving time in Strangeways Prison in Manchester, but she didn't know what for. Anyway, he was coming out today.

"I'm sure it can't be for something wicked," she told herself.

She had missed him. The house in Cheetham Hill felt empty and lonely without him around. They had lived together for decades in their late parents' shabby house, since they had all arrived from Dvinsk, Russia.

Morris came out of prison. Rosie cooked for him.
"Nice evening, Morris," said Rosie at the dinner table.
"Could be better, Rosie. This lokshen soup* is salty, but the fish isn't bad. Ta."
And that was as far as she got at finding anything out.
"I'm off out for a while," said Morris, dropping his napkin onto his plate. "Don't wait up for me. I'll be back late."

"Are you going far, Morris?"
"Nah!" he laughed. "Put the radio on for company, if you like. Toodle-oo."
"But you've just come back. What are you up to?"

Rosie and Morris slipped back easily into their routine.
"I can't believe you've ever been away," she told him the next morning.
"I'm off to work, Rosie," he said, slamming the front door behind him.

*A traditional Jewish dish made from chicken and noodles

As far as Rosie was concerned, Morris was going to work, as usual, in the family scrap rags and metal business in Mary Street, with brother Joseph.

While he was out, she cleaned the threadbare house as best she could. Mice were her biggest problem. No matter how many traps she set to catch them, they seemed to be thriving. Rosie's other job was shopping and cooking for her brother. For that, Morris gave Rosie housekeeping money and a bit extra for treats.
She loved buying clothes from Kendal Milne* which she kept in boxes, covered in tissue paper.
"I'll lose weight so I can wear them," she told herself, but she never did.

Life was back to normal. Morris was out all day every day.
Most evenings he would eat and then go out to meet up with other men - or so he said.

*A department store in Manchester

One evening months later, Morris was out as usual after his supper, when there was a loud banging on the front door. Rosie didn't open it.

Who the heck would be coming round at this time? she thought.

The banging continued.

"What do you want? Who are you?" she shouted.

"I've come for Morris. I have something for him. Let me in and I'll wait for him. He's expecting me."

The man had a deep voice with a strong Manchester accent.

"You must have heard my name, Jack?" he said.

"Jack, eh? Have I heard that name before?"

She went to the door, opened it on the security chain and peeped out.

The security chain snapped! Jack had shoved his whole weight against the door. He was in the house with an iron bar in his hand.

"Where's the bleeding bastard? He told me he would have something for me to collect."

"Morris, Morris? I don't know where he is," said Rosie.

He was so big he blocked the light out from the window above the door.

"You're a bleeding liar," he snarled.

And then he smashed the iron bar down on her head.

She shrieked, but no one heard her. He whacked her again.

"Tell your brother that there won't be a next time."

It was the neighbours who called the police. Rosie had stumbled out of the house and managed to knock on their door. Confronted with a woman covered in blood, they shut the door and called for help.

II

Morris arrived home to discover that Rosie wasn't there, but policemen were rummaging around the house. "Your sister is in Crumpsall Hospital. She'll survive - needs a few stitches in her head," a sergeant told him. "She can't remember too much. She said that Jack did it and maybe you know him?"

"Nah, I don't know any Jack who would beat my sister up."

"We think your sister's a fence*. How did she get all these boxes filled with expensive clothes from Kendal Milne?"

"I don't know. I've never seen them before," said Morris.

For the first time, Morris had a glimpse of Rosie's dreams.

*A person who deals in stolen goods